JUNIE B. JONES
IS ON HER WAY

From The Chicken House

Junie B. never puts a foot wrong – usually it's a whole leg! She's the funniest, bravest, truest small girl ever.

Barry Cunningham
Publisher

JuNie B. JONeS
IS ON HeR Way

By Barbara Park
Illustrated by Denise Brunkus

2 Palmer Street, Frome, Somerset BA11 1DS

To Cody –
who missed his bus and inspired this book

First published in the United States in 1992 by Random House, Inc.
as 'Junie B. Jones and the Stupid Smelly Bus'

Text copyright © 1992 by Barbara Park
Illustrations copyright © 1992 by Denise Brunkus

This edition first published in Great Britain in 2006 by
The Chicken House
2 Palmer Street
Frome, Somerset BA11 1DS
United Kingdom
www.doublecluck.com

Cover design by Radio
Cover Illustration by Denise Brunkus
Typeset by Dorchester Typesetting Group Ltd
Printed and bound in Great Britain

1 3 5 7 9 10 8 6 4 2

British Library Cataloguing in Publication data available.

10 digit ISBN 1 905294 06 9
13 digit ISBN 1 978 1905294 06 0

Contents

Chapter 1

Meeting Mrs

My name is Junie B. Jones. The B stands for Beatrice. Except I don't like Beatrice. I just like B and that's all.

I'm almost five years old.

Almost five is when you get to go to school. School is where you go to meet new friends and not watch TV.

Today was my first day. I'd been to my room before, though. Last week Mother took me there to meet my teacher.

It was called Meet the Teacher Day. My

teacher was decorating a display board with the letters of the alphabet.

'I already know all of those letters,' I said. 'I can sing them. Except I don't feel like it right now.'

My teacher shook my hand. Only our hands didn't fit together that good.

Her name was Mrs— I can't remember the rest of it. Mrs said I looked sweet.

'I know it,' I said. 'That's because I have on my new shoes.'

I held my foot way up high in the air.

'See how shiny they are? Before I put them on, I licked them.'

'And guess what else,' I said. 'This is my bestest hat. Grampa Miller bought it for me. See the devil horns sticking out at the sides?'

Mrs laughed. Except I don't know why. Devil horns are supposed to be scary.

Then we walked around the room and she showed me where stuff was. Like the easels where we get to paint. And the shelves where the books are. And the tables where we sit and don't watch TV.

One of the tables in the front of the room had a red chair. 'I would like to sit here, I think,' I told her.

But Mrs said, 'We'll have to wait and see, Junie.'

'B!' I said. 'Call me Junie *B*.!'

I yelled the B part really loud. So she wouldn't forget it.

People are *always* forgetting my B.

Mother rolled her eyes and looked at the ceiling. I looked up there, too. But I didn't see anything.

'Are you going on the mini-bus, Junie B.?' Mrs asked me.

I made my shoulders go up and down. 'I don't know. Where's it goin' to?'

My mother nodded her head and said, 'Yes, she'll be going on the bus.'

That made me feel scary inside. 'Cos I never rided on a bus before.

'Yeah, only where's it goin' to?' I asked again.

Mrs sat on her desk. Then she and my mother talked more about the bus.

I tapped on Mrs.

'Guess what? I still don't know where it's goin' to.'

Mrs smiled and said the bus driver's name was Mr Woo.

'Mr Woo,' said Mother. 'That's an easy name for Junie B. to remember.'

I covered my ears and stamped my foot.

'YEAH, ONLY WHERE'S THE

STUPID SMELLY BUS GOIN' TO?'

Mother and Mrs frowned.

Frowning is when your eyebrows look grumpy.

'Watch yourself, Madam,' said Mother. Madam's my name when I'm in trouble.

I looked down at my shoes. They didn't look as shiny as they did before.

Just then another mother and a boy came in. And Mrs went off to talk to them instead of me. I don't know why, though. The boy was hiding behind his mother and acting very babyish. I can beat that boy up, I think.

After that, my mother sat me down and explained about the bus. She said it's yellow. And it's called school mini-bus. And it stops at the end of my street.

Then I get on it. And sit down. And it takes me to school.

'And then your teacher will meet you in the car park,' said Mother. 'OK, Junie B.? Won't that be fun?'

I nodded the word *yes*.

But inside my head I said the word *no*.

Chapter 2

Feeling Squeezy

I stayed scared about the bus for a whole week. And last night when my mother tucked me into bed, I still felt sickish about it.

'Guess what?' I said. 'I don't think I want to go on that mini-bus to school tomorrow.'

Then my mother rumpled my hair. 'Of course you do,' she said.

'Of course I don't,' I said back.

Then Mother kissed me and said, 'It'll be fun. You'll see. Just don't worry.'

I did, though. I worried very much. And I

didn't sleep very good, either.

And this morning I felt very droopy when I got up. And my stomach was squeezy. And I couldn't eat my cereal.

And so I watched TV until Mother said it was time to get ready to go.

Then I put on my skirt that looks like velvet. And my new fuzzy pink jumper. After that, Mother and I walked to the corner to wait for the bus.

And guess what? There was another mother and little girl there, too. The little girl had curly black hair . . . which is my favourite kind.

I didn't say hello to her, though. 'Cos she was from a different street, that's why.

Then finally this yellow mini-bus came around the corner. And the brakes screeched very loud. And I had to cover my ears.

Then the door opened.

And the bus driver said, 'Hi! I'm Mr Woo. Hop on!'

Except I didn't hop on. 'Cos my legs didn't want to.

'I don't think I want to go on this bus to school,' I told Mother again.

Then she gave me a little push. 'Go on, Junie B.,' she said. 'Mr Woo is waiting for you. Be a big girl and get on.'

I looked up at the windows. The little girl with the curly black hair was already in the bus. She looked very big sitting up there. And kind of happy.

'Look how grown-up *that* little girl is acting, Junie B.,' said Mother. 'Why don't you sit next to her? It'll be fun. I promise.'

And so I got on the bus.

And guess what?

It wasn't fun.

Chapter 3

The Stupid Smelly Bus

The mini-bus wasn't like my daddy's car at all. It was very big inside. And the seats didn't have any cloth on them.

The little curly girl was sitting near the front. And so I tapped on her.

'Guess what?' I said. 'Mother said for me to sit here.'

'No!' she said. 'I'm saving this seat for my best friend, Mary Marble!'

Then she put her little white bag on the place where I was going to sit.

And so I made a face at her.

'Hurry up and find a seat, young lady,' said Mr Woo.

And so I quick sat down across from the curly mean girl. And Mr Woo shut the door.

It wasn't a normal kind of door, though. When it closed, it made a whishy sound.

I don't like that kind of door. If it closes on you by accident, it will cut you in half, and you will make a squishy sound.

The bus made a big roar. Then a big puff of black smelly smoke came out of the back end of it. It's called bus breath, I think.

Mr Woo drove for a while. Then the brakes made that loud, screechy noise again. I covered my ears so it couldn't get inside my head. 'Cos if loud, screechy noises get inside your head, you have to take an aspirin. I saw that on a TV advert.

Then the bus door opened again. And a dad and a boy with a grouchy face got on.

The dad smiled. Then he plopped the grouchy boy right next to me.

'This is Jim,' he said. 'I'm afraid Jim isn't too happy this morning.'

The dad kissed the boy goodbye. But the boy wiped it off his cheek.

Jim had on a rucksack. It was blue.

I love rucksacks. I wish I had one of my very own. One time I found a red one in a rubbish bin. But it had a little bit of gushy on it, and Mother said no.

Jim's rucksack had lots of zippers. I touched each one of them.

'One . . . two . . . three . . . four,' I counted.

Then I unzipped one.

'HEY! DON'T!' yelled Jim.

He zipped it right up again. Then he

moved to the seat in front of me.

I hate that Jim.

After that, the bus kept stopping and starting. And lots of children kept getting on. Loud children. And some of them were the kind who look like meanies.

Then the bus began getting very noisy and hot inside. And the sun kept shining down on me and my fuzzy hot jumper.

And here's another hot thing. I couldn't roll down my window because it didn't have a handle. And so I just kept on getting hotter and hotter.

And it smelled in the bus, too. The bus smelled like an egg salad sandwich.

'I want to get off of here,' I said right out loud. But nobody heard me. 'I hate it in this stupid smelly bus.'

Then my eyes got a little bit wet. I wasn't

crying, though. 'Cos I'm not a baby, that's why.

After that, my nose started running. Only the bus didn't have a glove compartment. Which is where you keep the tissues, of course. And so I had to wipe my nose on my fuzzy pink jumper sleeve.

Then I stayed on the bus for about an hour or three. Until finally I saw a big playground.

That meant we were at school!

Then Mr Woo drove the bus into the car park and stopped.

I jumped up very fast. 'Cos all I wanted to do was get off that stupid smelly thing!

Only guess what? That Jim pushed right in front of me. And the curly mean girl did, too. And then people started squishing me really tight. And so I pushed them away. And

they pushed me right back.

That's when I fell down! And a big foot stepped on my skirt that looks like velvet.

'STOP IT!' I yelled.

Then Mr Woo shouted, 'HEY, HEY, HEY!'

And he picked me up. And helped me off the bus.

Mrs was waiting for me just like my mother said.

'Hello there! How lovely to see you!' she called.

Then I ran over to her. And I showed her the big footprint on my skirt that looks like velvet.

'Yeah, only look what happened. I got stepped on and so now I'm dirty.'

Mrs brushed it. 'Don't worry, Junie,' she said. 'It'll come off.'

After that I just folded my arms and made a frown.

'Cos guess what?

She forgot my B again.

Chapter 4

Me and Lucille and Some Others

Some of the other bus children turned out to be in my class, too.

One of them was that Jim.

That Jim I hate.

Mrs made us line up. Then we followed her to our room. Its name is Room Nine.

There were other children waiting by the door. When Mrs unlocked it, everyone squeezed in all at once.

That Jim stepped on my new shoe. He made a scratch mark on my shiny toe. The kind of scratch that licking won't fix.

'HEY! WATCH IT, YOU DUMB JIM!' I shouted at him.

Mrs bent down next to me. 'Let's try to use our quiet voice while we're in school,' she said.

I nodded nicely. 'I hate that Jim,' I said in my quiet voice.

After that, Mrs clapped her hands together very loud.

'I want everyone to find a chair and sit down as fast as they can,' she said.

That's when I ran to the table with the red chair. Only guess what? There was already someone sitting there! A girl with little red fingernails.

And so I tapped on her and said, 'I would

like to sit there, I think.'

'No,' she said. '*I* am."

'Yeah, only I already picked that chair out,' I told her. 'Ask my mother if you don't believe me.'

But the girl just shook her head no.

And then Mrs clapped her loud hands again and said, 'Please find a seat!'

And so then I had to quick sit down in a stupid yellow chair.

The same stupid colour as the stupid yellow mini-bus.

After that, Mrs walked to a big cupboard in the back of the room. It's called the stationery cupboard. She got out boxes of new pointy crayons and some white circles. Then she passed them out. And we had to print our names on the circles and pin them to our fronts.

It was our first work.

'If you need help spelling your name, raise your hand,' said Mrs.

I raised my hand.

'I don't need help,' I told her. 'Grandma Miller says I print beautifully.'

I used red. But then a mistake happened. I made my **JUNIE** too big and there wasn't any room left for my **B**. And so I had to squish it very teeny at the bottom.

'I HATE THIS STUPID DUMB

CIRCLE!' I yelled.

Mrs made the *shhh* sound and gave me a new one.

'Thank you,' I said nicely. 'Grandma Miller says I print beautifully.'

The girl with the little red fingernails was faster than me. She showed me her circle and pointed to her letters.

'L-U-C-I-L-L-E. That spells *Lucille*,' she said.

'I like that name of Lucille,' I said. ''Cos guess why? Seals are my favourite animals. That's why.'

Then Mrs passed out drawing paper. And we drew pictures of our family.

Mrs put a happy-face sticker on mine.

It was very good. Except I made my father too tiny. And Mother's hair looked like sticks.

After that, Mrs took our class on a walk around the school. Everyone had to find a partner to walk with.

My partner was Lucille. We held hands.

The boy I can beat up was right in front of us. His partner was that Jim.

That Jim I hate.

The first place we walked to is called the Media Centre. My mother calls it a library. It's where the books are. And guess what? Books are my very favourite things in the whole world!

'HEY! THERE'S A JILLION OF THEM IN HERE!' I yelled, feeling very excited. 'I THINK I LOVE THIS PLACE!'

The librarian bent down next to me. She said to use my quiet voice.

'YEAH, ONLY GUESS WHAT? RIGHT NOW I JUST LIKE THE KIND OF BOOKS WITH PICTURES. BUT MOTHER SAYS WHEN I GET BIG, I'M GOING TO LIKE THE KIND WITH JUST WORDS. AND ALSO, TINNED TOMATOES.'

The boy I can beat up said, 'Shhh.'

I made a fist at him.

Then he turned around.

After that, we went to the dinner hall. The dinner hall is where children eat lunch. It is just like a restaurant. Except no menus, and no waiters. Plus you have to eat whatever they give you.

'Ummm!' I said. 'It smells yummy in here! Just like pasta and meatballs!'

Then that Jim turned around and held his nose.

'Poo . . . I smell *you*,' he said.

Lucille laughed very hard.

And so I stopped holding her hand.

The next place we went to was the nurse's office.

It's very nice in that place. There are two little beds where you get to lie down. And two little blankets that are the colour of tartan.

Our nurse doesn't look like a nurse. She doesn't wear white clothes and white shoes.

Our nurse is just a normal colour.

Lucille put up her hand. 'My brother said that last year he came here. And you let him take off his shoes. And he got a drink of water in just his socks!'

That Jim turned around again.

'Poo . . . I smell your feet,' he said to Lucille.

This time Lucille stuck out her tongue at him.

After that, we held hands again.

Chapter 5

Headteacher

After we left the nurse, we went to the main office. That's where the boss of the school lives. His name is Headteacher.

Headteacher is a baldy.

He talked to us.

Then Lucille put up her hand. 'My brother said that last year he had to come down here. And you shouted at him. And now he's not allowed to beat up other children at playtime any more.'

Headteacher kind of laughed. Then he

held the door for us to leave.

After that, we walked to the water fountain. And Mrs let us get a drink. I didn't get a long one, though. 'Cos people kept tapping on me.

'Hurry up, girl,' they said.

'Yeah, only guess what? That's not even my name,' I told them.

'Her name is Junie Bumblebee,' said Lucille.

Then she laughed. But I didn't think it was a very funny joke.

After that, Mrs showed us where the toilets were.

There's two kinds of toilets in our school. A boys' kind. And a girls' kind. I can't go in the boys' kind, though. 'Cos no girls allowed, that's why.

I tried to peek my head in there. But Mrs snapped her fingers at me.

The only boy who got to go into the toilet was the boy I can beat up. He was jiggling around very much.

Then he started running all over the place. And he was holding the front of his trousers.

'William!' said Mrs. 'Are you having an emergency?'

Then William yelled, 'YES!' And he ran right in there.

The rest of us walked back to our room.

I touched Lucille's fingernails. She said that her fingernail polish is named Very Very Berry.

'I would like to have my fingernails red, too,' I said. 'But I'm only allowed to have the kind of polish that makes them look shiny. Its name is Clear. Clear is the colour of spit.'

'I hate Clear,' said Lucille.

'Me too,' I told her. 'And also I hate yellow – which is the colour of the stupid

smelly school mini-bus.'

Lucille nodded her head. 'My brother said when you go home on the mini-bus, kids pour chocolate milk on your head.'

Then all of a sudden my stomach felt very squeezy again. 'Cos I had to go home on the bus, that's why.

'Why did you have to tell me that for, Lucille?' I said kind of grouchy.

After we got back to Room Nine, we did some more work. It was a game to help us learn each other's names.

I learned Lucille. And also a girl named Charlotte. And another girl named Grace. Then I learned a boy named Ham – which we eat at Grandma Miller's.

Pretty soon Mrs clapped her loud hands together.

'OK, everyone. Gather up your things.

It's almost time for the bell.'

Then I heard a noise in the car park. It was screechy brakes. And so I looked out the window. And I saw the school mini-bus.

It was coming to get me!

'Oh no!' I said sort of loud. 'Now I'm going to get chocolate milk poured on my head!' Then I chewed on my fingers.

'Get in line! Get in line!' said Mrs. 'When we get outside, I want all of the bus children to come with me. The rest of you must go to the lollipop lady.'

Everyone was lining up. I was the very last one.

Just then the bell rang and Mrs marched out of the door. Then everybody else marched out, too.

Except guess what?

I didn't.

Chapter 6

A Good Hider

When you're the very last one in line, nobody watches you. That's how come nobody saw me when I ducked behind the teacher's desk and hid.

I'm a good hider.

One time at Grandma Miller's house, I hid under the kitchen sink. Then I made a growly sound and sprung out at her.

I'm not allowed to do that any more.

Anyway, I stayed scrunched behind the teacher's desk for a while. And then I saw a better place to hide. It was the big stationery cupboard in the back of the room.

And so I ran back there very fast. And I squeezed onto the bottom shelf. I squeezed right on top of the coloured paper.

Most of me was comfortable. Except my head was sort of very tight. And my knees were all bended. Like when I do a somersault.

Then I pulled the door mostly closed.

'Don't shut it all the way, though. And I *mean* it,' I said right out loud.

I stayed really quiet for lots of minutes. Then I heard noises in the corridor. And some feet came running into the room. Big people's feet, I think.

'What happened?' I heard someone ask.

'I've lost one of my little girls,' said a voice that sounded like Mrs. 'Her name is Junie B. Jones. And she didn't get on the bus. So now we've got to go out looking for her.'

Then I heard some keys jingle. And the feet went running out again. And then the door shut.

I still didn't come out of the cupboard, though. When you're a good hider, you can't come out for a very, very long time.

I just stayed there all bended up. And I told myself a story. Not an out-loud story. I just told it inside my head. It was called 'The Little Hiding Girl'.

I made it up. And this is how it went:

Once upon a time there was a little hiding girl. She was in a secret spot where nobody could find her. Except her head was very tight. And her brain was squishing out.

But she still couldn't come out of her spot. Or a smelly yellow monster would get her. And also, some meanies with chocolate milk.

The end.

After that, I rested my eyes.

Resting your eyes is what my grampa does when he watches TV after dinner. Then he snores. And Grandma Miller says, 'Go to bed, Frank.'

It's not the same thing as a nap, though.

'Cos naps are for babies, that's why.

And anyway, I didn't snore. I just did a little dribble.

Then finally when my eyes had finished resting, they woke up.

And so I came out of the cupboard and ran right up to the window. And guess what? There weren't any cars in the car park. And no stupid smelly bus, either!

'Whew! That's a relief,' I said.

A relief is when your stomach doesn't feel squeezy any more.

After that, I went back to the cupboard. 'Cos while I was hiding, I sniffed the smell of plasticene, that's why. And plasticene is my very favourite thing in the whole world!

'Hey! I see it up there!' I said.

The plasticene was on the middle shelf. I stood on a chair to get it.

It was blue and stiff. And so I had to roll it on the floor to make it soft and warm. Then I rolled it into a blue orange. It was very beautiful. Except it had some dirt and hair on it.

After I had finished, I went to the front of the room and sat down in my teacher's big chair. I like teachers' desks very much. The drawers are so big I could fit in one, I think.

I opened up the top one. There were happy-face stickers. And rubber bands. And also, gold stars – which I love a very lot.

I stuck one on my forehead.

Then I found paper clips. And red marking pens. And new pencils with no points. And scissors. And tissues. And guess what else?

'Chalk!' I said. 'Brand-new chalk that's not even out of its little box yet!'

Then I stood up on my teacher's chair and clapped my hands together very loud.

'I want everyone to find a chair and sit down! Today we are going to learn some alphabet and some reading. And also, I will teach you how to make a blue orange. But first, everyone has to watch me draw stuff.'

Then I went to the board and drew with my brand-new chalk. I drew a bean and a carrot and some curly hair.

Then I wrote some **O**'s.

O's are my bestest letter.

After that, I bowed. 'Thank you very much,' I said. 'Now you may all go out for playtime . . .'

I smiled.

'Except for not that Jim.'

Chapter 7
Peeky Holes and Spying

After a while, I started to get a little bit thirsty. That's what happens when chalk sprinkles get in your throat.

'I would like a drink of water, I think,' I said.

Then I put my hands on my hips. 'Yeah, only what if somebody sees you at the water fountain? Then they might call the stupid smelly bus to come and get you. And so you better not go.'

I stamped my foot. 'Yeah, only I *have* to go! 'Cos there's stupid chalk in my throat!'

Then all of a sudden I got a great idea! I pulled a chair over to the door. And I peeked out of the window at the top!

I'm a good peeker.

Once I peeked right into Grampa Miller's mouth when he was sleeping. And I saw that dangly thing that hangs down in the back. I didn't touch it, though. 'Cos I didn't have a little stick or anything, that's why.

Anyway, I didn't see anybody in the hall. And so I opened the door a crack. And I sniffed. 'Cos when you sniff, you can smell if there's people around.

I learned sniffing from my dog, Tickle. Dogs can smell everything. People can mostly just smell big smells. Like stink and flowers and dinner.

'Nope. Don't smell anyone,' I said.

Then I ran to the water fountain and I drank for a long time. And nobody tapped on me and said, 'Hurry up, girl.'

After that, I stood on my tip-toes. And I tippy-toed to the Media Centre. 'Cos I love that place! Remember?

The Media Centre is kind of like a fort. The shelves are like walls. And the books are sort of like bricks. And you can move some of them around and make peeky holes.

Peeky holes are what you spy out of.

Then if you see somebody coming, you can make your breath very quiet. And they won't find you.

I spied for a long time. But nobody came. The only people in the Media Centre were just me and some fish.

The fish were in a big glass tank. I waved at them in there. Then I stirred them with a pencil.

I love fish very much. I eat them for dinner with coleslaw.

Just then I saw my most favourite thing in the whole world! Its name is an electric pencil sharpener! And it was sitting right on the librarian's desk!

'Hey!' I said very excited. 'I think I know how to work that thing!'

Then I looked in the desk drawer. And guess what? There were lots of brand-new pencils in there!

And so I sharpened them!

It was funner than anything! 'Cos an electric pencil sharpener makes a nice noise. And you can make pencils as teeny as you want. You just keep pushing them into the little hole. And they just keep on getting teenier and teenier.

It doesn't work on crayons, though. I tried a red one. Then the pencil sharpener slowed right down. And then it made a *rrrrr-rrrrr* sound. And after that, it didn't go any more.

Just then I heard a noise! It was walking feet. And it made me scared inside. 'Cos I didn't want anyone to find me, that's why!

And so I squatted right down and looked through my peeky hole.

Then I saw a man with a rubbish bin! He was singing 'Somewhere Over the Rainbow.' That's a song I know. It's from my favourite film, which is called *The Wizard of Odds*.

The man with the bin didn't see me. He walked down the corridor. Then I heard him go outside. I stayed squatted down for a long time. But he never came back.

'Whew! That was a close one!' I said.

And so then I ran to find a better place to hide.

Chapter 8

The Dangerous Nurse's Office

Guess where I ran to? Straight to the nurse's office, of course! 'Cos there's those little tartan blankets to hide under!

There's other great stuff in there, too. Like some scales to weigh yourself. And a sign with a giant **E** and other letters.

The nurse uses the sign to test your eyes. She points to the letters. And you have to shout out their names.

You have to shout the **E** the loudest. That's how come it's so big.

And guess what else I saw in the nurse's office? Plasters, that's what! I love those things!

They were on top of the desk. And so I opened the lid. And I sniffed them.

'Mmmm,' I said. 'Cos plasters smell just like a brand-new beach ball.

Then I tipped them out. They were the most prettiest plasters I ever saw! They were red and blue and green! And also yellow. Which is the colour I hate.

And they were different shapes, too. There were squares and circles. And some were that very long kind – which are called butterflies, I think.

I put a green circle on my knee. That's where I fell down on the pavement last week.

It's mostly all better now. But if I press it very hard with my thumb, I can still make it hurt.

After that, I put a blue butterfly strip on my finger. That's where I got a splinter from the picnic table. Mother pulled it out with tweezers. But there's still some table in there, I think.

Also, I put a red square on my arm. That's where Tickle scratched me. Because I got him all wound up.

Just then I saw the nurse's purple cardigan. It was hanging on her chair.

I put it on.

'Now I'm the nurse,' I said.

Then I sat down. And I pretended to call the hospital.

'Hello, hospital? It's me, the nurse. I need some more plasters and some aspirins and some cherry throat sweets. Only not the kind that make your mouth feel freezy.

'And I need some lollipops for when children get needles.

'And also I need a little stick or something in case I have to touch that dangly thing that hangs down in your throat.'

Then I pretended to call Room Nine.

'Hello, Mrs? Please send that Jim to my office. I have to give him an injection.'

Just then I saw my most favourite thing in the whole world! They were near the door. And their name is crutches!

Crutches are for when you break a leg. Then the doctor puts it in a big white cast with just your piggies sticking out. And you can't walk on it. And so she gives you crutches to swing yourself.

I ran over and picked them up. Then I put them under my arms. Only they were much

too long for me. And I didn't swing that good.

And so then I got another idea! I carried them to the nurse's chair. And I climbed up there so I was really tall. And then I put the crutches under my arms. And they fitted just right!

After that, I stood on the edge of the chair. And I leaned forward very slow.

Except then a terrible thing happened! The chair was on wheels. And it rolled away from my feet! And I got stuck on the crutches high up in the air! And I was very dangly up there!

'HEY!' I shouted. 'GET ME DOWN FROM HERE!'

Then I wiggled around. And one of the crutches slipped. And I came crashing down! And I banged my head on the desk!

'OW!' I yelled. 'OW! OW! OW!'

Then I picked up the phone again. 'I'm leavin' this stupid job!' I said.

And then I ran out of there very fast.

'Cos the nurse's office is a dangerous place.

And crutches aren't my favourite thing any more.

Chapter 9

Zooming Speedy Fast

I like running inside the school.

It's funner than running inside your house. In school you can zoom with your arms out like a plane. And you don't knock over the furniture. And also the head doesn't get broken off your mother's bird statue. Which used to be a blackbird, I think.

I zoomed straight to the dinner hall. 'Cos there's a lot of tables to hide under in that place. Only when I tried to open the door, it was all locked up!

And so then I ran to another room across the corridor. Only that stupid door was locked, too!

'Hey! Who did all this dumb locking?' I asked.

Then I started jiggling up and down. 'Cos I was having a little bit of a problem, that's why. The kind of problem that's called *personal*.

And it's about going for a you know what.

And so all of a sudden I had to run down the corridor speedy quick!

Right to the girls' toilets!

Only guess what? When I got there, *that* stupid door wouldn't open, either!

And so I kicked it. And I hanged on the handle. 'Cos I weigh seventeen kilos.

'OPEN UP AND I MEAN IT!' I yelled.

But the door kept on staying shut!

'IT'S A 'MERGENCY!' I shouted.

And then all of a sudden I remembered about that boy I can beat up! 'Cos *he* had a 'mergency, too! And *he* got to go into the *boys'* toilets!

And so I zoomed across the hall. And I pulled on the boys' toilet door. But that stupid dumb thing was locked, too!

'STUPID, STUPID DOORS!' I yelled.

After that, I started to jiggle up and down very fast. 'OH, NO! NOW I'M GOIN' TO HAVE AN ACCIDENT ON MY SKIRT THAT LOOKS LIKE VELVET!'

Only just then I remembered something *else* about 'mergencies. 'Cos Mother told me what to do if I ever needed help.

And its name is Call 999!

And so then I ran back to the dangerous nurse's office. 'Cos that's where the phone was, of course! And then I picked it up. And I pushed the 9! And 9 again! And again!

'HELP! THIS IS A 'MERGENCY!' I yelled. 'ALL THE DOORS ARE LOCKED IN THIS PLACE! AND NOW I'M GOING TO HAVE A TERRIBLE ACCIDENT!'

Then I heard a voice on the other end. She said for me to calm down.

'YEAH, ONLY I CAN'T! 'COS I'M IN BIG TROUBLE! AND I'M ALL BY MYSELF! AND I NEED HELP REALLY BAD!'

Then the lady said to calm down again. Except for I couldn't stand still! And so I just hung up and ran right out of there.

And I just kept running and running till I got to the big doors at the end of the corridor.

And then I runned right outside! 'Cos maybe there might be a little toilet out there or something.

Except I didn't see one. All I could hear was sirens! Loud sirens were all over the place.

And they kept on getting closer and closer! And then a big red fire engine came zooming right around the corner! And a white police car! And a fast green and yellow ambulance!

And guess what else? They turned right

into the school car park!

And so I stopped jiggling for a second. And I sniffed the air. Only I couldn't smell any smoke!

Then I heard a grouchy voice. 'HEY! HOLD IT, MADAM!' it yelled.

And I got very scared inside. 'Cos Madam's my name when I'm in trouble.

I turned around. It was the man with the bin! And he was running at me!

'HOLD IT RIGHT THERE!' he shouted again.

And then I started to cry.

'Yeah, only that's the trouble. I can't hold it!' I said. 'I already holded it all I can! And now I'm having a 'mergency! And all the toilets are locked! And now I'm going to have an accident very quick!'

And then the man with the bin didn't look so grouchy any more.

'Well, why didn't you say so?' he said.

Then he pulled a big bunch of keys out of his pocket. And he grabbed my hand.

And then him and me zoomed back into the school! Speedy fast!

Chapter 10

Me and That Grace

The man with the bin unlocked the girls' toilets for me. And I ran right in there.

And guess what? I made it! That's what! I didn't have an accident on my skirt that looks like velvet!

'Whew! That was a close one!' I said.

Then I washed my hands at the basin. And I looked in the mirror. And the gold star was still on my forehead!

It looked very beautiful up there!

After that, I went into the corridor and

the man with the bin bended down to me.

'Everything OK, sweetheart?' he said.

And so I nodded my head. 'I holded it,' I said very happy.

Then all of a sudden there were lots of people running at us.

There were firemen. And policemen. And there was a tall lady rolling a bed on wheels.

'Hey!' I said to the man with the bin. 'What happened? Did somebody get runned over in here or something?'

Then I saw Mrs and Headteacher and Mother. They were running at us, too.

And then Mother bended down and hugged me very tight!

After that everyone started talking at once. And nobody was using their quiet voices. And nobody was smiling either.

Headteacher started asking me a jillion

questions. Mostly they were questions about hiding in the stationery cupboard.

'I'm a good hider,' I told him.

Headteacher acted a little bit grumpy. He said I wasn't allowed to do that any more.

'When you go to school, you have to follow the rules,' he said. 'What would happen if every boy and girl hid in the stationery cupboard after school?'

'It would be very smushy in there,' I said.

Then he made his eyes frowny. 'But we wouldn't know where anyone was, would we?' he said.

'Yes,' I said. 'We would all be in the stationery cupboard.'

Then Headteacher looked up at the ceiling. And I looked up, too. But I didn't see anything again.

After that, Mother looked at my plasters.

'Did you hurt yourself?' she asked.

And so I told her all about the dangerous nurse's office. And then I showed her the nurse's purple cardigan. And she made me give it back.

After that, everybody started leaving. The firemen. And the policemen. And also the tall lady with the bed.

Then finally, my mother got to take me home. And guess what? I didn't have to ride on the stupid smelly bus.

Except the car wasn't that fun. 'Cos Mother was grouchy at me.

'I'm sorry the bus wasn't fun for you, Junie B.,' she said. 'But what you did was very, very wrong. Didn't you see all the commotion you caused? You had a *lot* of people very scared.'

'Yes, but I didn't want chocolate milk

poured on my head,' I explained to her.

'That's *not* going to happen,' growled Mother. 'And you can't just suddenly decide for yourself not to go on the bus. *Hundreds* of children go to school on buses every day. And if they can do it, you can do it, too.'

Then my eyes got wet again. 'Yeah, but there's meanies on that thing,' I said all sniffly.

Then Mother stopped being so growly.

'What if you had a friend to sit with?' she said. 'Your teacher told me there's a girl in your class who will be going on the bus for the first time tomorrow. Maybe you could sit together. Would you like that?'

I made my shoulders go up and down.

'Her name is Grace,' said Mother.

'Grace?' I said. 'Hey! I know that Grace! I learned her today!'

And so when we got home, Mother called

that Grace's mother. And then they talked. And then me and that Grace talked too. I said hi and she said hi. And she said she would sit with me.

And so tomorrow I get to take my little red bag on the bus. And I get to put it on the seat next to me so nobody will sit there.

Nobody except for that Grace, of course.

And then she and me might get to be friends. And we can hold hands. Just like me and Lucille.

I will like that, I think.

And guess what else?

Tomorrow I think I might like yellow a little bit, too.

About the Author

"I never missed the bus on purpose," says Barbara Park. But she admits that she did go to the Headteacher's office for talking too much in class. "It's funny," she adds, "because now Headteachers actually *want* me to come and talk in their classrooms!"

The author of lots of hilarious books for young readers, Barbara Park has received many awards, including seven *Children's Choice* awards and four *Parents' Choice* awards. She lives in Arizona with her husband, Richard, and their two sons, Steven and David.

Read this next book about me. And I mean it!

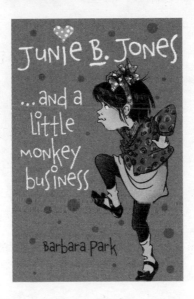

The bestest girl is back

The school office is a scary place.
It has loud ringing phones. And a typing lady who is a stranger.
And a row of chairs where bad children sit.

   Mrs plopped me in a blue one.
   "Wait here," she said.
   "Yeah, only I'm not bad," I whispered to just myself.
   Then I put my jumper on my head. So nobody would see me
in the bad person's chair.